Enid Blyton's

NODDY

and the Pouring Rain

BBC BOOKS

It was raining. It wasn't at all the sort of morning for driving around the wet roads of Toyland.

"Parp! Parp!" said Noddy's car, miserably.

"Yes, it's a horrid day," said Noddy. "Perhaps we should stay at home."

At that moment, Big-Ears arrived. He was carrying two umbrellas.

"Hello, Big-Ears," said Noddy. "Have you come for a ride?"

"No. I've come to lend you my old umbrella so you won't catch a cold in the rain," said Big-Ears kindly.

"Your *old* umbrella," sniffed Noddy. "Won't
you need it to keep your new umbrella dry?"
But Big-Ears insisted that Noddy take it.
Noddy thought it would be rather awkward,
but at last he set off to find some passengers.

Martha Monkey was in the town square. She wanted to go to the station. She got into the car and flopped her tail on Noddy's knee.

"Please have your wet tail back," said Noddy. And he shoved Martha Monkey's tail into her basket.

"You're wetting the cakes I'm taking to my aunt!" exclaimed Martha. "I'll hold your umbrella for you."

"Thank you," said Noddy. But Martha held the umbrella over herself.

"This is cosy," she said, while poor Noddy got wetter and wetter.

At the station Martha Monkey got out of Noddy's car.

"Come back at 5 o'clock to take me home," she ordered. "And don't you dare be late!"

"I hate rainy days," said Noddy. "They make everyone grumpy and miserable."

Then Mrs Tubby Bear and a sulky-looking
Master Tubby Bear appeared. Mrs Tubby Bear
was so pleased to see Noddy that he cheered
up at once. And soon he was driving the
Tubby Bears home.

But Master Tubby was being naughty. He started to wiggle the umbrella. And then he shoved the umbrella right over Noddy's eyes. "*Stop* it!" yelled Noddy. "I can't see where I'm going."

The very next minute, Noddy's car crashed straight into a letter-box. The letter-box tumbled over and started to roll off down the street.

"Oh, no!" shouted Noddy, pushing the umbrella aside. "Come back, letter-box!"

Noddy set off after the rolling letter-box. It
was scattering Toy Town in every
direction. The Clockwork Mouse
leapt out of the way and was left
hanging from a lamp-post. He
squeaked in alarm.

The letter-box rolled on. It headed straight
for Mr Jumbo. And he fell backwards, right into
the fruit stall. Down it crashed. Oranges,
apples and tomatoes went rolling in every
direction.

Noddy was still trying to catch up with the letter-box.

"Stop! Come back," he yelled. Then the Skittle family dashed in front of the rolling letter-box to be knocked down.

"Whee!" they squeaked. "We love falling over."

Mr Plod was standing outside his police station. "At last," he said. "The rain seems to be stopping." Just then he heard a terrible, rumbling, rolling noise. "Oh, my word," said Mr Plod, as the letter-box barged into him and knocked him flat.

Just as Mr Plod scrambled to his feet, Noddy turned up. Mr Plod was angry.

"What do you know about this runaway letter-box, Noddy?" he asked sternly.

"It wasn't Noddy's fault," said Mrs Tubby Bear.

"It was Big-Ears' old umbrella," said Noddy.
"I couldn't see. And that letter-box bumped into
my car."

"Sounds like dangerous driving to me," said
Mr Plod. "You must not drive for one whole
day, Noddy."

"Oh, no!" cried Noddy. "I need my car. Everyone wants rides today."

But the policeman took no notice. "I shall keep your car at the police station. You can collect it tomorrow," he said firmly.

Poor Noddy. He ran off with the umbrella.

"You'll have to get out, Mrs Tubby Bear," said Mr Plod. "Come along, car."

But Noddy's car set off all by itself, in the opposite direction.

"Parp! Parp!" it said, while Mr Plod watched in amazement.

Big-Ears was knocking on Noddy's front
door, just as Noddy's little car arrived with the
Tubby Bears.

"Noddy's car has come home to look for
him," said Mrs Tubby Bear. "But I'm afraid
Noddy has run away."

"Tell me what's happened," said Big-Ears.

Meanwhile, Noddy stumbled along carrying the umbrella. "I knew I hated rainy days," he said. "I didn't mean to knock the letter-box over. It was all that rain, and Big-Ears' silly old umbrella."

At the station, the train was ready to leave.
"All aboard," shouted the driver. Then Noddy trudged on to the platform. He wasn't looking where he was going, and he walked straight into the train. BUMP!

"What's the matter, Noddy?" asked the train driver, kindly. Noddy told him what had happened. "It wasn't my fault," he said, "but now I can't drive my car for a whole day."

"Don't worry," said the driver. "You can help us at the station. We need an extra porter today."

Meanwhile, Big-Ears searched everywhere for Noddy. "Have you seen him?" he asked Mr Sparks, at the garage.

"No," said Mr Sparks. "And now *I've* got to drive all his passengers."

"Please look out for him," said Big-Ears, anxiously.

Noddy enjoyed being a porter. "Toy Town! Toy Town!" he yelled, waving his umbrella as the train came in.

"You're a good porter," smiled the driver. "But this is the last train today."

"Well, I'll go and see who else I can help," said Noddy busily.

Outside the station, Martha Monkey waited impatiently for Noddy's car to arrive. But when Noddy did appear he told her he couldn't take her home.

"What use is a taxi driver who can't drive?" snorted Martha Monkey.

"I'm a porter now," said Noddy, proudly. "I can carry your basket."

"All right," said Martha, crossly. "Pick it up."

But while Noddy was talking he didn't see his umbrella handle pick up the basket.

"Where has my basket gone?" asked Martha.

"It can't be far away," said Noddy, hopefully.

"It's full of special biscuits from my aunty," said Martha, anxiously.

They looked all around, but they couldn't see the basket. It was hanging behind Noddy on the end of the umbrella.

Noddy was puzzled. "It's not here," he said. "It's gone," wailed Martha. Then Noddy noticed the umbrella felt very heavy. He swung it round, and there was Martha's basket! Martha Monkey was not pleased.

Just then, Mr Sparks arrived in his car. He was relieved to see Noddy. "Quick, jump in," he said. "Mrs Tubby Bear has baked you a special apple pie." They drove off at top speed. But poor old Big-Ears didn't see them go, as he arrived wearily at the station, still in search of Noddy.

At House-for-One everyone ate up Mrs Tubby's delicious apple pie. Suddenly there was a knock on the door. Martha Monkey hurried to open the door and was surprised to find a very tired Big-Ears, standing on the door-step.

"Big-Ears!" cried Noddy.

"Oh, Noddy," said Big-Ears. "I've been looking everywhere for you."

"I'm sorry," said Noddy. "I've had a lovely day with your old umbrella."

There was nothing poor Big-Ears could say to that, was there?

Other Noddy *TV Tie-in titles*
available from BBC Children's Books

Noddy and his Bell
Noddy and the Goblins
Noddy Loses Sixpence
Noddy and Martha Monkey
Noddy and the Naughty Tail
Noddy and his New Friend
Noddy and the Kite

Other TV Tie-in titles in preparation

Noddy and the Broken Bicycle
Noddy Delivers Some Parcels
Noddy Gets a New Job
Noddy and the Milkman
Noddy and the Special Key

Published by BBC Books
a division of BBC Enterprises Limited
Woodlands, 80 Wood Lane, London W12 0TT
First published 1992
Reprinted 1992
Text and stills copyright © BBC Enterprises Limited 1992
ISBN 0 563 36855 1

Based on the Television series, produced by
Cosgrove Hall Productions, inspired by the Noddy Books
which are copyright Darrell Waters Limited 1949-1968

Enid Blyton's signature and Noddy are Trademarks of Darrell Waters Limited

Designed and typeset in 17/21pt Garamond by Between the Lines, London

Printed and bound in Great Britain by Cambus Limited, East Kilbride
Colour separations by DOT Gradations, Chelmsford
Cover printed by Cambus Limited, East Kilbride